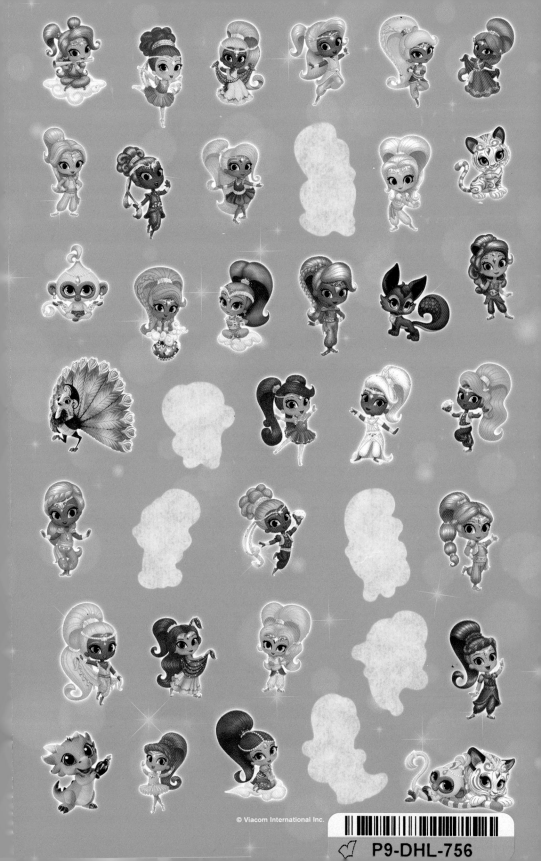

P9-DHL-756

Teenie Genies

Collector's Guide

Written by **Kristen Yu-Um**

Illustrated by **Victoria Miller and Dave Aikins**

Random House 🏠 New York

randomhousekids.com
ISBN 978-1-5247-1919-7
Printed in the United States of America
10 9 8 7 6 5 4 3 2

Boom, Zahramay! Up and away!

Grab your magic carpet and take a ride through a genie wonderland, where friendships and adventures await! **F**ollow the sparkles through **Z**ahramay **F**alls and discover genies of every kind racing on flying carpets, baking yummy treats, playing with their adorable pets, having tea parties, and using their special genie magic to make everything more fun!

Friends Divine

**Shimmer and Shine, your genies divine!
Magical friendships, one of a kind!**

Shimmer

Shimmer is always excited about . . . well, just about everything— especially if lots and lots of glitter is involved! She is super sweet and loves giving hugs. Her playful pet monkey, Tala, is often at her side. Or on her shoulder. Or on her head.

Personality: Cheerful, giggly, upbeat

Pet: Tala

Loves: Everything!

Quote: "I love it!"

Fun Fact: Shimmer loves to clean!

Shine

It's like she always says: "When in doubt, just follow the sparkles!" Older than her twin sister, Shimmer, by one minute, Shine has plenty of words of wisdom . . . that she makes up on the spot! She is fearless, funny, and bubbling with confidence. Shine loves animals, especially her pet Bengal tiger cub, Nahal.

Personality: Brave, bold, witty

Pet: Nahal

Loves: Taking chances

Quote: "That's 'cause I just made it up!"

Fun Fact: She loves telling silly jokes.

Tala

Tala is Shimmer's playful pet monkey. Tala loves shiny things and playing dress-up! She is very curious and loves to go on adventures with her best genie friend.

Personality: Goofy, lovable, curious

Loves: Climbing, shiny objects

Secret Talent: Juggling pineapples

Nahal

Nahal is Shine's super-cute Bengal tiger cub. She can be a bit of a scaredy-cat when it comes to loud noises, but she is still the *purr*-fect pet and playtime companion!

Personality: Silly, feisty, cautious

Loves: Pouncing, belly rubs

Favorite Activity: Snuggling with Shine

Leah

Leah is patient, fun, kindhearted, courageous, and most importantly . . . Shimmer and Shine's best human friend! She loves having twin genies to grant her wishes. And she loves seeing and trying all kinds of new things in Zahramay Falls!

Loves: The magic genie bottle necklace that calls her genies, the special genie outfit she wears when visting Zahramay Falls

Favorite Ballet: Swan Lake

Hobbies: Baking, bowling, skateboarding, playing video games

Quotes: "I have an idea!"

Fun Fact: Leah and her best friend, Zac, have watched *The Dragon Princess* movie 135 times!

10

Parisa

Leah's pet fox, Parisa, is pretty and purple. Even though she has a more serious side, she happily joins in on Nahal and Tala's mischief-making fun.

Personality: Playful, smart, reserved

Loves: Making her tail really fluffy

Special Power: Can change the color of her fur to blend into her environment

Princess Samira

Princess Samira is the kindest and most powerful genie in all of Zahramay Falls! As mentor to every wish-granting genie, she is always busy helping someone learn a new *genie*-rific skill. Samira's favorite feathery friend is a peacock named Roya.

Personality: Kind, generous

Loves: Inventing new challenges for the genies-in-training

Favorite Place: Her palace

Quote: "Time to poof!"

Zeta

Zeta is a troublemaking sorceress whose goal is to become more powerful than anyone else in Zahramay Falls. Her plans include dreaming up new ways to steal Genie Gems and making special potions to stop the genies and their magic. Zeta became a sorceress when she dropped out of genie training.

Personality: Sneaky, jealous, tricky

Loves: Making magic potions to trick people

Special Accessories: Crystal ball, flying scooter

Favorite Place: Her secret lair

Quote: *"Zip, zow! Open now!"*

Roya

Princess Samira's pet peacock acts like true royalty.

Personality: Proud, fancy

Loves: Samira's attention, fancy masquerade balls

Special Power: Once a year, Roya loses a single feather that can repair a broken object.

Nazboo

Nazboo is Zeta's loyal pet dragon. Whenever the sneaky sorceress is riding on her scooter, Nazboo is right next to her in the sidecar. Though he does his best to help Zeta on her missions, Nazboo is usually focused on finding his next snack!

Personality: Cuddly, quirky, funny

Favorite Food: Anything he can get his hands on!

Special Power: When Zeta's not looking, Nazboo likes to play with Tala and Nahal.

Rainbow Sparkle

Greens and reds, yellows and blues,
genies sparkle in magical hues!

Odara

Favorite Color:
Red

Hobby:
Apple-picking with Nevina

Favorite Treat:
Doubly-Bubbly bubble gum

Prized Possession:
Ruby-red shoes

Zareen

Secret Talent:
Can change into any
color of the rainbow

Fashion Style: Dazzling

Hobby: Ice dancing

Quote:
"It's crystal clear to me!"

Anarosa

Favorite Gem: Jade

Favorite Food: A big bowl of greens

Loves: Playing dress-up with Aubria

Favorite Book: *Green Means Glow!*

Orinda

Personality:
Encouraging, imaginative

Favorite Plant:
Lavender

Prized Possession:
Purple Pixie Powder

Minal

Favorite Drink:
Pink lemonade

Favorite Flower:
Flamboyant fuchsias

Favorite Treat:
Doubly-Bubbly bubble gum

Quote:
"I'm tickled pink!"

Aubria

Favorite Gem:
Emerald

Loves:
Playing dress-up with Anarosa

Favorite Food:
Key lime pie

Nevina

Personality:
Sassy, strong, smart

Hobby:
Exploring genie caves with Odara

Favorite Color:
Scarlet

Favorite Dessert:
Strawberry Sparkle Soufflé

20

Jenina

Favorite Gem: Purple opal

Favorite Lip Gloss: Very Violet

Favorite Dessert: Fancy floating figs

Tamsin

Favorite Gem: Sapphire

Favorite Food: Blueberry muffins

Prized Possession: Sparkly blue shoes

Tava

Favorite Scent: Fresh-cut grass

Hobby: Climbing trees without using magic

Favorite Color: Moss green

Favorite Genie Gem: The Green Burst Gem, because it helps make grass grow super fast!

Keely

Personality:
Bubbly, helpful, generous

Favorite Scent:
Raspberry rainbow cookies

Quote:
"Have a *keely* nice day!"

Orli

Favorite Flower:
Orchids

Biggest Oopsie:
Reversing the rainbow!

Favorite Dessert:
Perfect Plum Cake

24

Kamaria

Favorite Lip Gloss: Very Cherry

Hobby: Watching fireworks

Nickname: Little Red

Quote: "Always *Red*-y to grant a wish!"

Genie Splash

Genies love to spend the day
playing by the sea.
With seashells, surf, and sand,
it's the place to be!

Nyssa

Hobby:
Surfing with Nerina

Can't Live Without:
Strawberry-scented sunscreen

Favorite Song:
"Hello, Wave!"

Hali

Favorite Animal:
Starfish

Hobby:
Collecting sand dollars

Favorite Tongue Twister:
"She sells seashells by the seashore."

Ziba

Favorite Flower: Sunflower

Favorite Place to Visit:
The Great Barrier Reef

Favorite Drink:
Super-sour lemonade

Meral

Favorite Color: Ocean blue

Hobbies: Swimming, snorkeling

Favorite Animal: Dolphins

Favorite Dance: The Swim!

Loralee

Personality:
Adventurous, energetic

Favorite Treat:
Saltwater taffy

Secret Talent:
Finding jewels at the bottom of the sea

Asami

Favorite Color:
Sea-foam green

Hobby:
Building sparkly sand castles

Prized Possession:
A giant pearl

Mira

Personality: Friendly, funny

Favorite Food: Raspberry ice pops

Quote: *"Sea you later!"*

Nerina

Favorite Game:
Beach Ball Bingo

Favorite Ice Cream Flavor:
Lemon-lime

Favorite Band:
The Three Wishes

Quote: "Sparkle Up!"

Mitra

Personality:
Charming, bright

Favorite Color: Sunset orange

Favorite Treat:
Tangy tangerine sherbet

Quote: "It's nice to *Mitra*!"

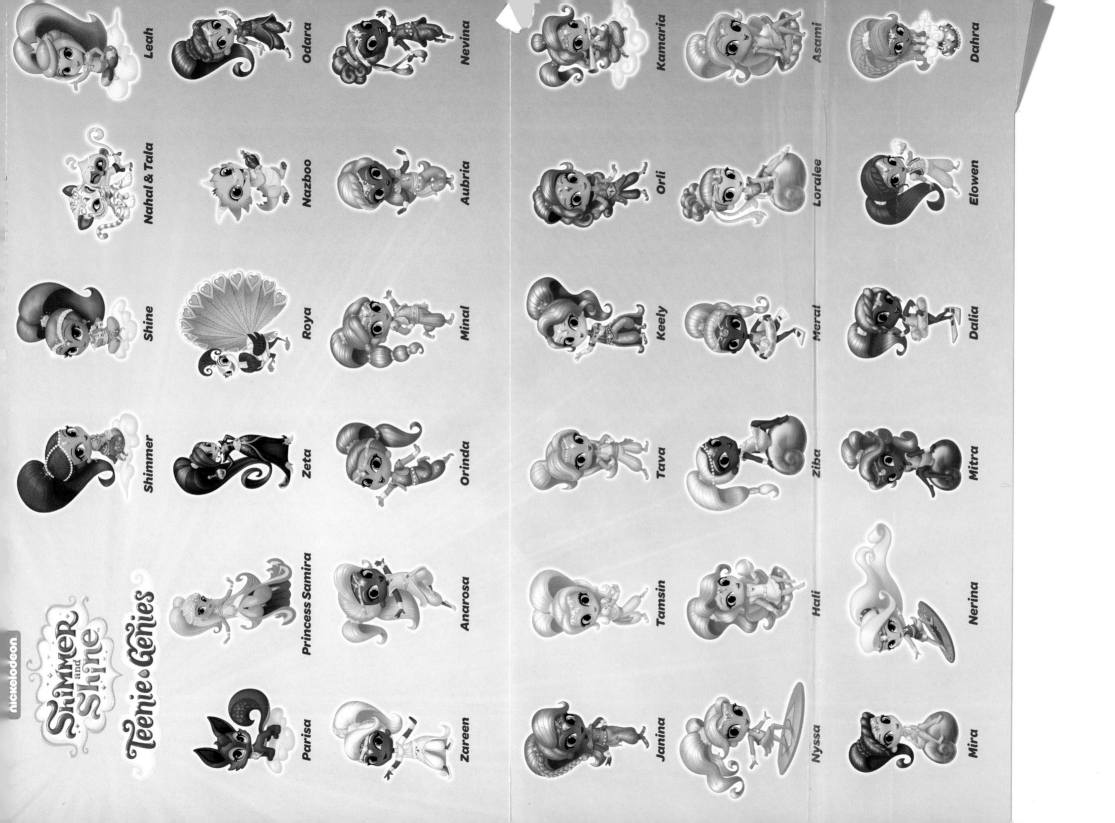

Leah

Odara

Nevina

Kamaria

Asami

Dahra

Nahal & Tala

Nazboo

Aubria

Orli

Loralee

Elowen

Shine

Roya

Minal

Keely

Merat

Dalia

Shimmer

Zeta

Orinda

Tava

Ziba

Mitra

Princess Samira

Anarosa

Tamsin

Hali

Nerina

Parisa

Zareen

Janina

Nyssa

Mira

SHiMMER and Shine

Teenie Genies

nickelodeon

Dalia

Special Talent: Plays the ukulele

Favorite Dance: The Hula Hop

Quote: "I'm feeling *beach*-y!"

Magical Market

If you've got a flying carpet,
here is a place to park it.
Genies can't resist a visit to the magic market!

Elowen

Favorite Shop in the Genie Market:
Fruit stand

Biggest Oopsie:
Baking too many
very berry cherry pies!

Quote:
"You're the *berry* best!"

Dahra

Personality:
Enthusiastic, cheery

Favorite Shop in the Genie Market:
Magic carpet stand

Hobby: Dancing

Secret Talent:
Hula-hooping while flying

Shayla

Loves:
Writing letters to Dahra

Hobby:
Glittery calligraphy

Likes Shopping For:
Sparkly pens, scented paper

Ahava

Secret Talent:
Meeting Fenella for tea and cookies in the marketplace

Favorite Wish Granted:
A polka-dotted pony!

Prized Possession:
Her purple scarf from Fenella

Fenella

Favorite Tea:
Magical Mint

Favorite Cookie:
Banana walnut

Prized Possession:
Her pink scarf from Ahava

Nabeela

Favorite Gem:
Diamond

Favorite Hobbies: Baking, decorating cakes

Favorite Thing to Bake:
Almond Cookie Cake

Felice

Favorite Shop in the Genie Market:
Yarn and fabric stall

Favorite Drink:
Pomegranate punch

Favorite Fabric: Shimmery satin

Quote: "Wink! Wink! What's your wish?"

Laleh

Favorite Shop in the Genie Market: Bookshop

Favorite Scent:
Vibrant Vanilla

Best Subjects in School:
Reading, writing

Quote: "I can go anywhere in a book!"

Farnaz

Favorite Shop in the Genie Market: The sparkly jewels stand

Favorite Color: Indigo

Likes: Helping others, making people laugh

Loves: Making glittery gifts for her friends

Quote: "Let's make it extra-super sparkly!"

Dance Party

Sparkle, giggle, leap, and prance!
Everyone's going to the genie dance!

Ceri

Favorite Music:
Classical

Favorite Ballet:
Gazellia

Favorite Dance Style: Anything ballet

Nena

Personality:
Playful, caring, silly

Loves: Chatting with
Cyma, Tamra, and Shayna

Favorite Dance:
The Twisty Tango

Zora

Loves:
Face-painting with Nura

Hobbies:
Dancing, painting

Favorite Dance:
The Foxtrot

Aishah

Personality:
Fun-loving, witty

Favorite Dance:
The Hustle-Bustle

Quote:
"Dance like no one is flying by!"

Cyma

Personality: Creative, imaginative, sharp

Favorite Dance: The Genie Jive

Prized Possession: Sparkly gem earrings

Quote: "Ain't no party like a genie party!"

Shirin

Biggest Oopsie: Conjuring up dance shoes for two left feet!

Signature Dance Move: The Cherry Bomb

Quote from Friends: "It's Shirin for the win!"

Tamra

Favorite Dance Style: Ballet

Signature Dance Move: The Tamra Twirl

Favorite Dance Joke: Q. What do you call a dancing lamb?
A. A *baa*-llerina!

Nura

Favorite Dance Style: Tap

Hobby: *Tapping* into her creative side!

Quote: "Dance your heart out!"

Shayna

Best Wish Granted: Glow-in-the-dark dance shoes

Favorite Dance Style: The Swanky Swing

Signature Dance Move: The Super Shayna Shuffle

Zayn

Nickname: Zany Zayn!

Favorite Dance Move: The Glitterbug Jitterbug

Favorite Place to Dance: The Crystal Ball

47

Music Divine

The genies are jamming with
Shimmer and Shine.
Together they're making
music DIVINE!

Farah

Favorite Snack:
Groovy grapes

Fashion Style:
Funky!

Quote from Friends:
"She's a sparkly strummer!"

Nelita

Personality:
Marches to the beat of her own drum

Favorite Wish Granted:
A Thanksgiving dinner complete with "drumsticks"

Quote:
"Drumroll, please!"

Sanaz

Personality: Outspoken, opinionated, optimistic

Special Talent: Performing in a band with Lecia and Ara

Biggest Oopsie: Accidentally setting off fireworks during a concert!

Lecia

Special Talent: Writing silly songs about her friends

Nickname: Lecia the Lyricist

Favorite Band: WHISH

Ranaa

Nickname: Ranaa the Rapper

Favorite Dance Joke:

Q. What did the scared kitty do when it saw a dog?
A. It *Ranaa*-way!

Ara

Nickname: Ara the *Ara*-mazing!

Special Talent: She can beatbox the entire alphabet!

Favorite Joke: Q. What kind of music are balloons afraid of?
A. Pop music!

Milena

Loves: Helping friends out of *treble*!

Dreams About: Being a rock star

Quote: "Stay tuned for your next wish!"

Mahira

Loves: Spotting shooting stars

Favorite Song: "Little Wishing Star"

Favorite Dessert: Apple-Dapple Drumcake

Hana

Fashion Style: Sassy but classy

Biggest Dream: To start a band called the Hana Bananas

Favorite Fairy Tale: The *Pied Piper*

Quote: "Stay sparkly and *flute*-iful!"

Dreamy Genies

The sun has gone to sleep,
and the time is coming soon
for genies to sweetly dream
beneath a magic moon.

Mahsa

Personality:
Chill

Can't Live Without: Her lullaby-playing night-light

Quote:
"Dream it! Wish it!"

Reesa

Known For:
Being a great listener

Loves:
Soft pajamas

Quotes:
"Dreams are sweeter when you fall asleep smiling!"

Aziz

Favorite Bedtime Story: "The Flying Carpet of Faraway Falls"

Favorite Lullaby: "Rock-a-Bye, Genie"

Biggest Dream: To be the best wish-granting genie she can be!

Nalah

Hobby: Sharing secrets with Calla and Razi

Secret Talent: Building pillow forts

Prized Possession: Her extra-fluffy elephant pillow!

Jelena

Known For: Spotting shooting stars

Favorite Song: "Little Wishing Star"

Quote: "Love you to the moon and back!"

Calla

Favorite Flower:
Night jasmine

Fashion Style:
Elegant

Quote:
"Calla you later!"

Nadia

Favorite Vacation Spot: Slumber land

Prized Possession:
Her stuffed animal,
Fluffy the Bunny

Quote:
"Dream BIG!"

Nalani

Favorite Movie: *Genies in Dreamland*

Favorite Place to Visit: Double Land

Quote: "Dare to live your dreams!"

Razi

Hobby: Sharing stories with Calla and Nalah

Known For: Being pillow-fight champion!

Favorite Things: Slumber parties, sleeping bags, hot cocoa with marshmallows

Prized Possession: Rose-gold earrings

Turia

Dream Vacation: A trip to the moon!

Can't Live Without: Her satin pajamas

Favorite Things: "Follow your dreams all the way to the stars!"

The stars are shining
over **Z**ahramay **F**alls,
and it's time to say goodbye.
But you can visit us again soon
to make more wishes
and meet new genie friends.